This book belongs to:

This paperback edition first published in 2012 by Andersen Press Ltd.
First published in Great Britain in 1980 by Andersen Press Ltd.,
20 Vauxhall Bridge Road, London SW1V 2SA.
Published in Australia by Random House Australia Pty.,
Level 3, 100 Pacific Highway, North Sydney, NSW 2060.
 Printed and bound in Singapore by Tien Wah Press.

10 9 8 7 6 5 4 3 2

British Library Cataloguing in Publication Data available.

ISBN 978 1 84939 467 3

This book has been printed on acid-free paper

NOT NOW, BERNARD

David McKee

ANDERSEN PRESS

"Hello, Dad," said Bernard.

"Not now, Bernard," said his father.

"Hello, Mum," said Bernard.

"Not now, Bernard," said his mother.

"There's a monster in the garden and it's going to eat me," said Bernard.

“Not now, Bernard,” said his mother.

Bernard went into the garden.

“Hello, monster,” he said to the monster.

The monster ate Bernard up, every bit.

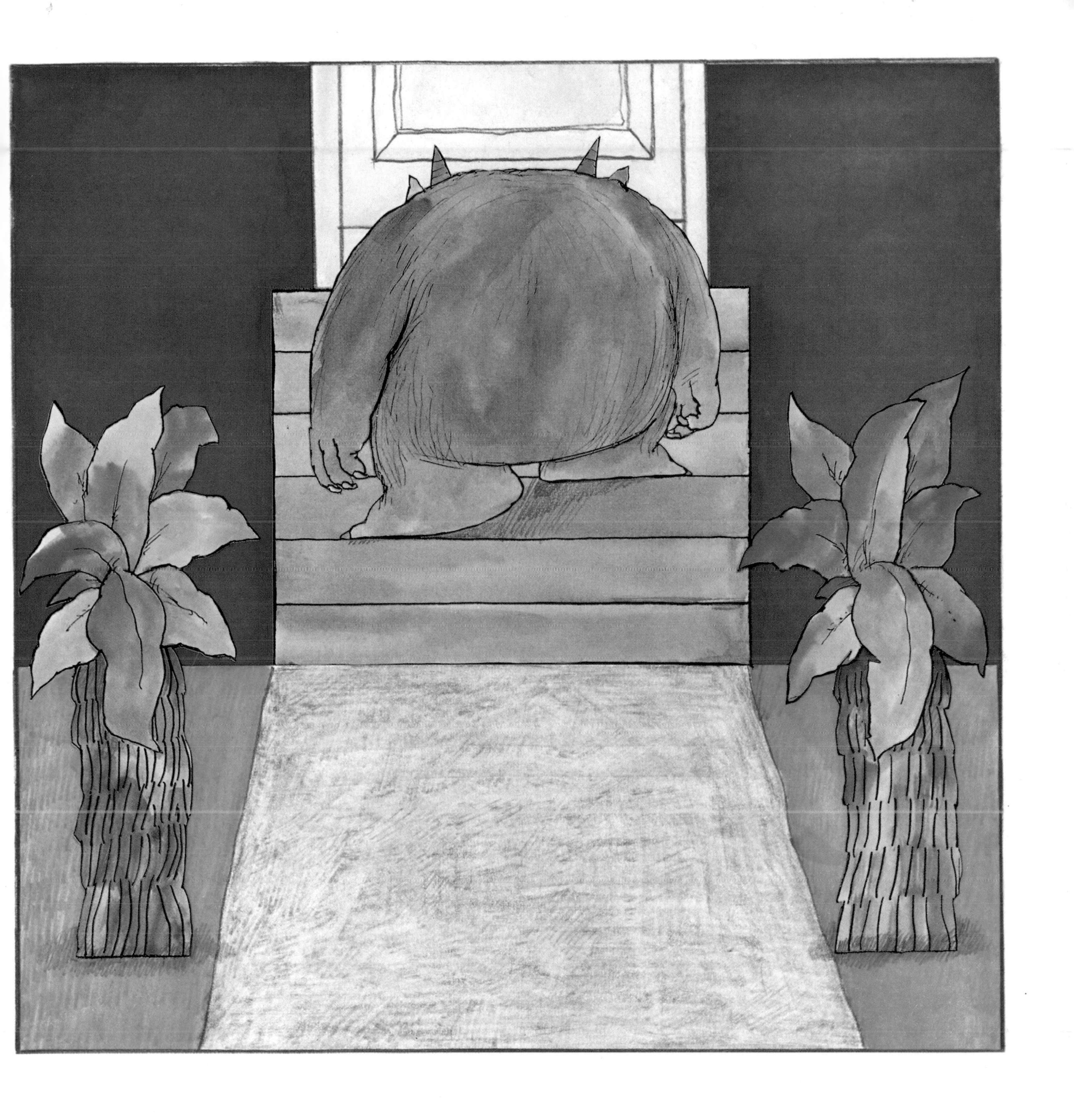

Then the monster went indoors.

"ROAR," went the monster behind
Bernard's mother.

"Not now, Bernard," said Bernard's mother.

The monster bit Bernard's father.

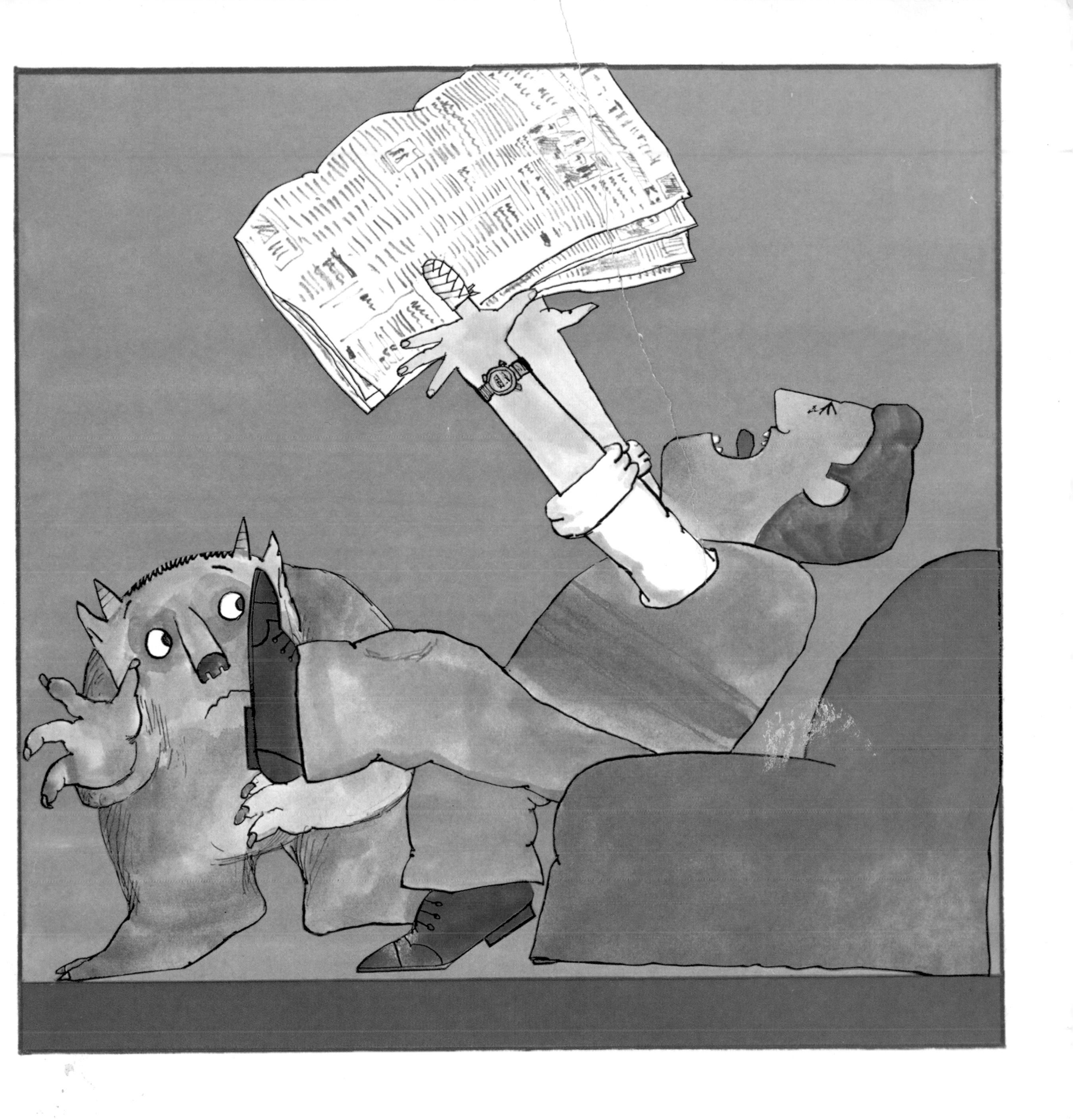

"Not now, Bernard," said Bernard's father.

"Your dinner's ready," said Bernard's mother.

She put the dinner in front of the television.

The monster ate the dinner.

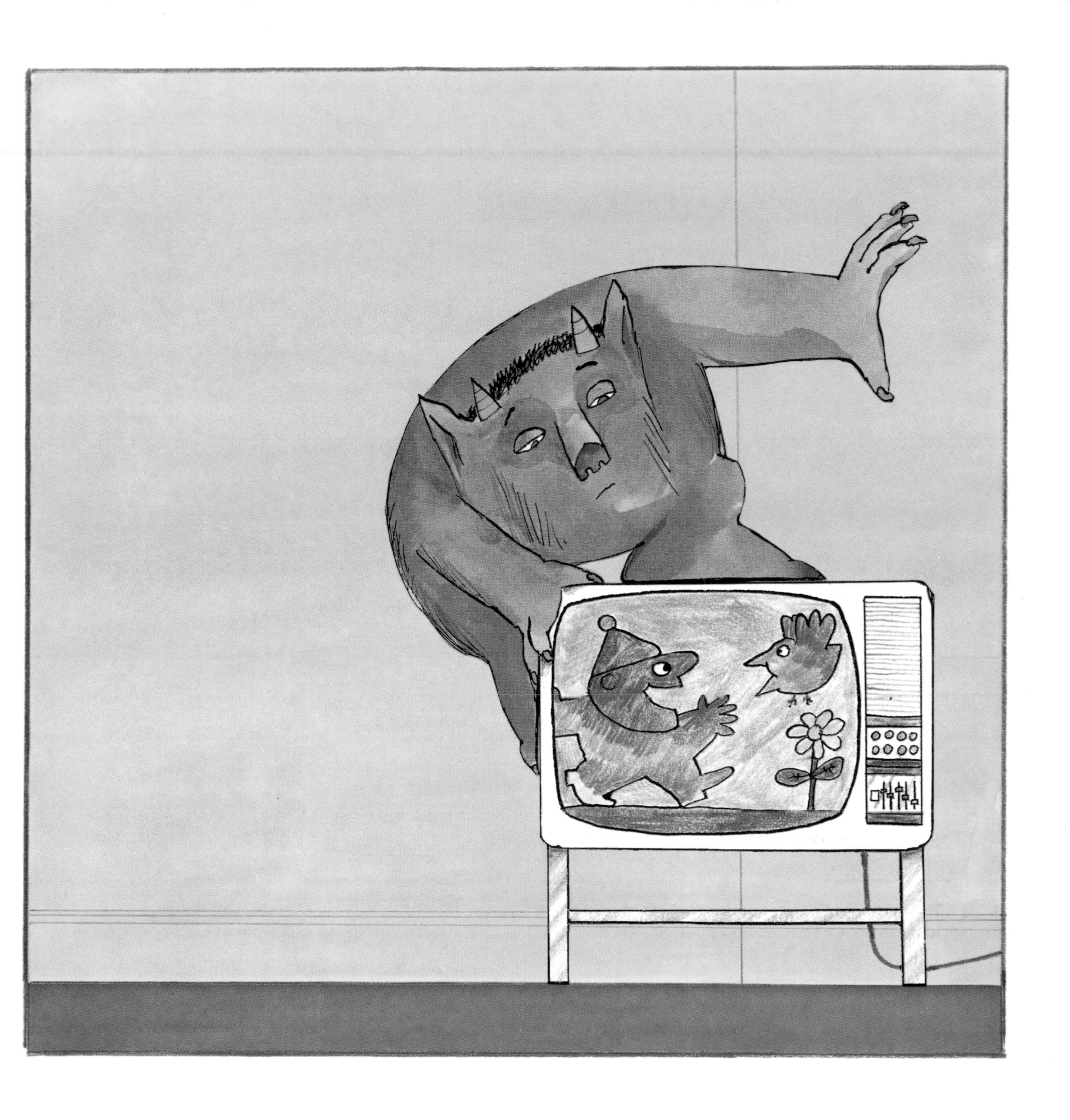

Then it watched the television.

Then it read one of Bernard's comics.

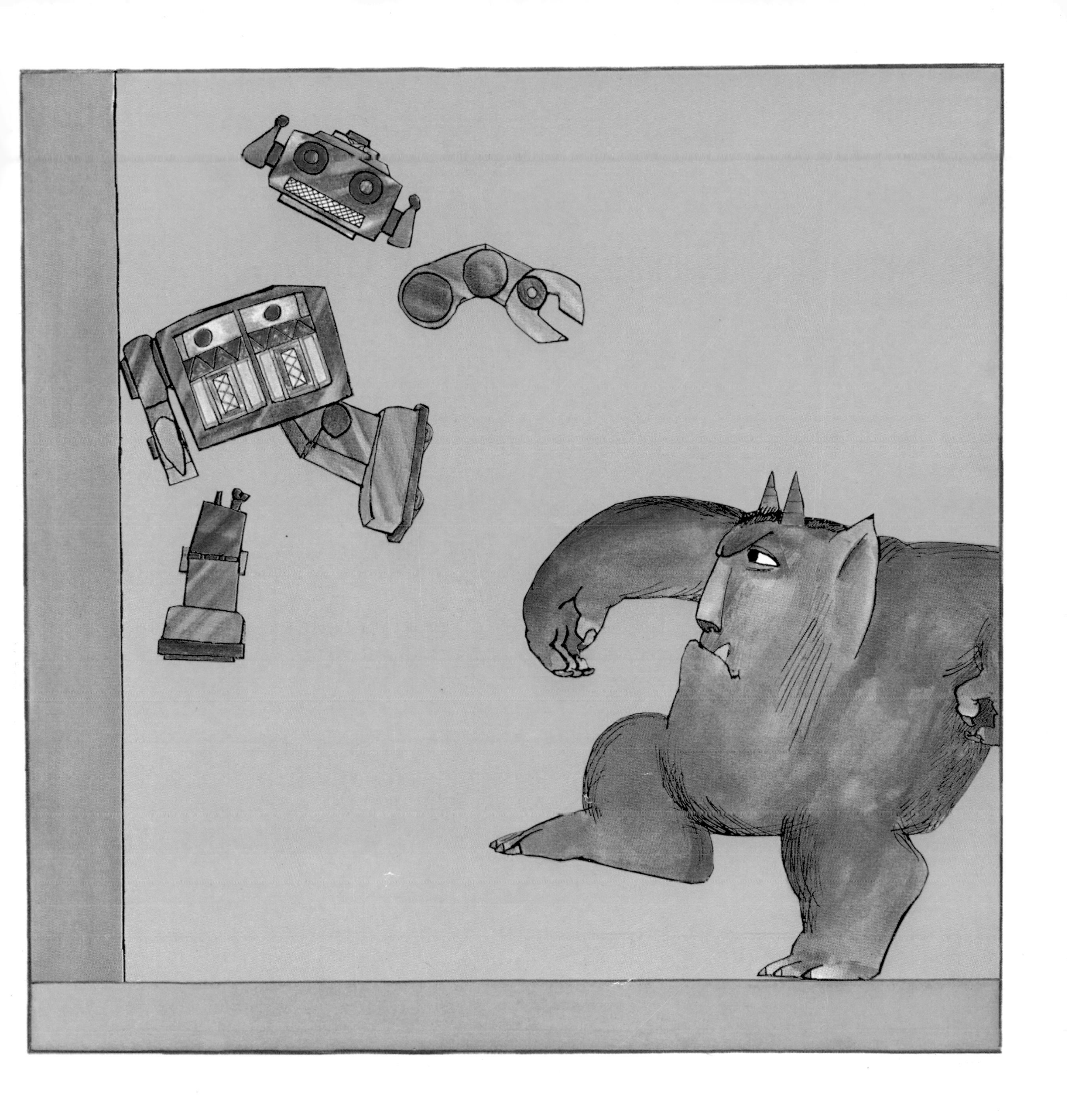

And broke one of his toys.

"Go to bed. I've taken up your milk," called Bernard's mother.

The monster went upstairs.

"But I'm a monster," said the monster.

"Not now, Bernard," said Bernard's mother.

Other books by David McKee:

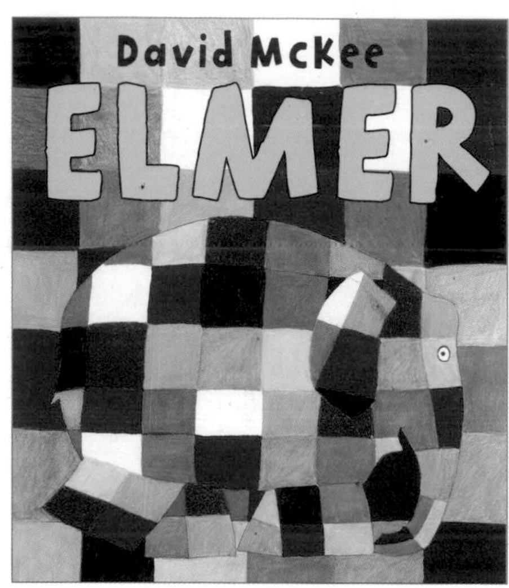

9781842707319 Also available as a book and CD

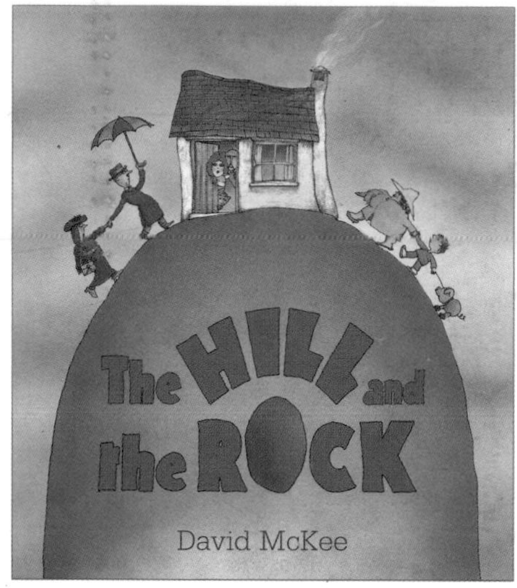

9781849393058

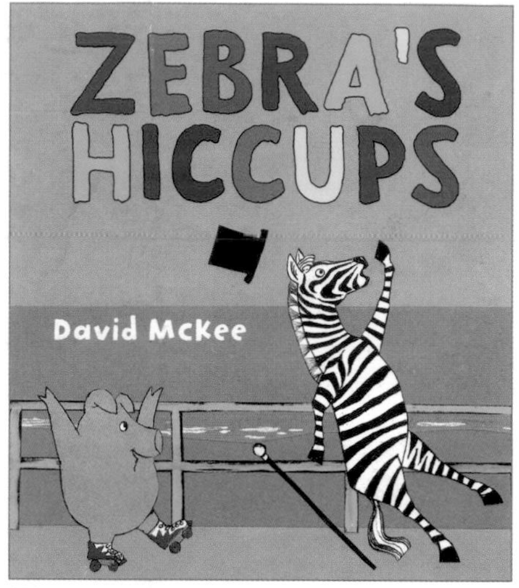

9781842709238

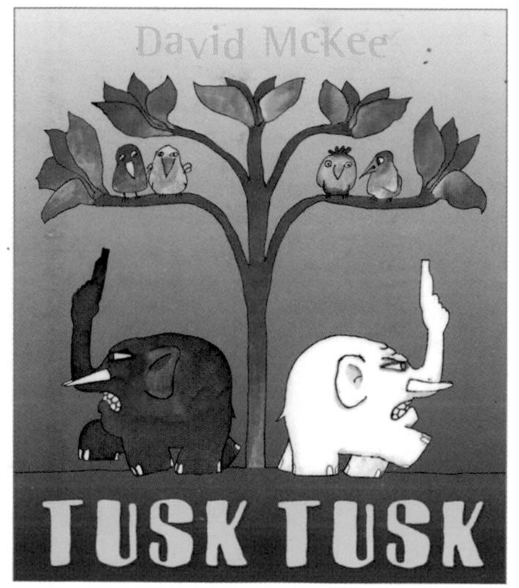

9781842705797

9781842704684

9781842708644